Shh!
Can you
keep a secret?

You're about to meet the
Ballet Bunnies, who live
hidden at Millie's ballet school.

Are you ready?

Tiptoe this
way . . .

Meet the Ballet Bunnies

Dolly

You'll never meet
a bunny who
loves to dance as
much as Dolly.

Fifi

If you're in
trouble, Fifi is
always ready to
lend a helping paw!

Pod

Pod loves to build
things out of the
bits and bobs he
finds. He also loves
his tutu!

Trixie

Yawn! When
she's not dancing,
Trixie likes curling
up and having
a nice snooze.

For Serenie Beans

OXFORD
UNIVERSITY PRESS

Great Clarendon Street, Oxford OX2 6DP
Oxford University Press is a department of the University of Oxford.
It furthers the University's objective of excellence in research, scholarship,
and education by publishing worldwide. Oxford is a registered trade mark
of Oxford University Press in the UK and in certain other countries

Text copyright © Swapna Reddy 2021
Illustrations copyright © Binny Talib 2021

The moral rights of the author/illustrator have been asserted

Database right Oxford University Press (maker)

First published 2021

British Library Cataloguing in Publication Data

Data available

ISBN: 978-0-19-277489-7

1 3 5 7 9 10 8 6 4 2

Printed in China

Paper used in the production of this book is a natural,
recyclable product made from wood grown in sustainable forests.
The manufacturing process conforms to the environmental
regulations of the country of origin.

Ballet Bunnies

The Big Audition

By Swapna Reddy

Illustrated by Binny Talib

OXFORD
UNIVERSITY PRESS

Chapter 1

'Watch MEEEEEE!' Fifi yelled.

The little bunny swung from the low hanging branches of the weeping willow tree. She let go of the branch and flew into a *grand jeté*, before landing in the soft grass by Millie.

'Oh, bunny fluff!' Pod exclaimed, his

long velvety ears standing tall. 'I want
to try that!'

Millie giggled as she watched her
four tiny bunny friends hop
towards the low branches,
all eager to fly
through the air.

For you and me, four talking, dancing bunnies swinging from a willow tree into *grand jetés* might seem a little odd. But for Millie, hanging out with the ballet bunnies from Miss Luisa's School of Dance was just another Saturday in the park.

'I have exciting news,' Millie said, as the bunnies bounced into a fluffy heap in the grass.

Dolly, Fifi, Trixie, and Pod hopped up on to Millie's lap as she leaned in close to talk to them.

'*Ballet Beat* is filming at Miss Luisa's School next week!' Millie squealed.

Millie and Mum loved *Ballet Beat*. It was their favourite TV show. They would cosy up on the couch to watch the famous dance show together every Sunday evening. They oohed and aahed over the sparkly costumes and the incredible acrobatic routines showcased each week.

'They're filming children from different dance classes for the very first time,' Millie continued, 'and they are looking for someone from *my* class to appear on the show!'

The bunnies looked up at Millie, wide-eyed with excitement.

'You would be brilliant on that show,' Pod said. 'They *have* to choose you.'

The bunnies nodded in agreement but Millie shook her head.

'I'm not good enough to audition,' Millie said.

'You won't know until you try,' Trixie said gently.

Millie screwed up her face.

'Trixie's right,' Dolly agreed.

Millie screwed up her face even tighter. 'I don't know,' Millie said slowly.

Seeing Millie's hesitation, Pod

hopped up on to her shoulder. 'What did your mum say?'

'I haven't told her I'm not going to audition,' Millie admitted.

'It might be a good idea to tell her how you feel,' Pod said gently.

Millie nodded. If anyone knew how much this would mean to Millie, it would be Mum.

Chapter 2

Millie got ready to pack up
the mini picnic that she had set up for
the bunnies, then she stopped.

'Hang on,' Millie said, looking
down at the bunnies. 'How come you
don't seem surprised to hear about
Ballet Beat?'

The four bunnies grinned at each other.

'We already knew!' Dolly squealed.

'What?' Millie gasped. 'How?'

'It's the talk of all the dance schools in town,' Fifi said.

Pod clapped his paws in excitement. 'Everyone's so excited about it.'

'*Everyone?*' Millie asked.

'We heard from the Ballet Bunnies at the dance school by the train station and *they* heard from Ballet Bunnies at the small studio by the mall,' Trixie piped up.

Millie's mouth hung open. *There were more Ballet Bunnies?*

'Oh, bunny fluff,' Dolly said to the others. 'I think Millie thought we were the *only* Ballet Bunnies around.'

The bunnies giggled as Millie shook her head in disbelief.

'We probably shouldn't mention the Hip Hop Hedgehogs and the Mambo Mice then,' Fifi whispered cheekily.

'Or the Bhangra Blue Jays,' Pod grinned back.

'I know all about bhangra,' Millie finally blurted out. 'My friend Samira taught me some moves.'

She whipped up her arms in the air, then shrugged her shoulders in time to the beat that Pod tapped out with his paws. Dolly, Fifi, and Trixie joined in, jumping next to Millie.

The bunnies stomped along until they were all exhausted and they collapsed in the grass.

'You know, you could meet the rest of the Ballet Bunnies if you wanted?'

Dolly suggested.

'Really?' Millie said, as she caught her breath. 'The others wouldn't mind?'

'Of course they wouldn't mind,' Fifi said. 'We've told them all about you and they can't wait to meet you.'

Millie blushed. She couldn't quite
get her head around the idea that every
dance studio had their very own family of
Ballet Bunnies. Or Hip Hop Hedgehogs
or Mambo Mice or Bhangra Blue Jays, as
it turns out.

Dolly bounced up into Millie's arms. 'We're having a talent show, here in the park, to celebrate *Ballet Beat* coming to town,' Dolly said to Millie. 'And you can be our guest of honour.'

Chapter 3

Millie tugged at Mum's
hand as they left the park for the dance
school.

'Mum! Everyone is so excited about
Ballet Beat coming to Miss Luisa's
school,' Millie said.

'Are you excited?' Mum grinned.

Millie nodded but Mum could see something was worrying her.

'Is everything OK, Millie?' Mum asked.

Millie took a deep breath. She remembered that Pod had said she should talk to Mum about her worries.

'There's going to be an audition and they're only going to pick one person and I'm not sure I'm good enough,' Millie blurted out.

'Oh, Millie,' Mum said, hugging her close.

Millie wrapped her arms around Mum tight. 'I'm not sure I'm as good as everyone else in my class,' she whispered.

Mum pulled away gently and gazed down at Millie. She smoothed back the stray strands of hair that had escaped from Millie's hair bun.

'All anyone can ask of you and all you can ask of yourself is to do your very best,' she said to Millie. 'I know how hard you're working on your ballet. And I know how much you love it. Give yourself a chance to show everyone how ballet makes you feel.'

When Millie was dancing, there was no better feeling in the world.

Mum smiled at Millie and Millie felt all her fears melt away. Mum was right. She would try her hardest and no matter what might happen she would always know she had done her best. That thought made her feel proud indeed.

◦ ✳ ◦

Miss Luisa showed the class the routine for the audition. It was more difficult than anything else they had ever been taught but the whole class was keen to learn. Millie was very impressed with everyone, especially Will. She couldn't help but stop in awe

to watch Will's clean spins
and effortless jumps.

'He's so good,' Samira said, stopping alongside Millie at the *barre*.

'I know!' Millie said. 'I can't wait to dance like that.'

'Neither of you will ever dance like that if you just stand around talking,' Amber smirked as she spun past them. 'Now move! You're in my way.'

Amber had never been very nice to Millie but today she was in a particularly mean mood.

'There's heaps of space to practice, Amber,' Samira said back, waving her arms around.

'This class should be for those of us who *actually* stand a chance of getting chosen for *Ballet Beat*,' Amber snarled. 'Those of you who would never make it should go and chat somewhere else,' she added, looking down her nose at Millie and Samira.

'Ignore her,' Samira said, squeezing Millie's hand as Amber *pirouetted* off to the other side of the studio.

Millie gave Samira a small smile. She wanted to ignore Amber's comments but they hurt.

Chapter 4

At the end of class, Millie grabbed her things and left the studio to wait for Mum in the foyer, where she noticed Amber in a corner.

As Millie stepped closer, she saw Amber's face fall. She recognized Amber's mum's voice. Amber and her

mum were talking but neither of
them looked very happy at all.

'No, you can't go to your friend's house this evening,' Amber's mum said.

'But—' Amber started.

'Or any other evening for that matter,' Amber's mum continued, her voice rising. 'You will be practising every evening until the day of the audition, do you understand, young lady?'

Amber's shoulders hunched forward and she hung her head and, though Millie couldn't quite see, she thought that Amber was crying.

'I don't want to hear any more of this,' Amber's mum went on. 'You *will* get that part, do you understand?'

'But what if I don't?' Amber said, her voice small.

'That's enough, Amber. We've spoken about this and there's no excuse for failure,' her mother replied. She turned on her heels and grabbed Amber's ballet bag. 'I'll see you by the car.'

Amber's mum brushed past Millie and strode out of the doors.

Amber was still staring at her feet as she brushed away tears from her wet cheeks. When she looked up, she saw Millie offering her a kind smile.

'What are you looking at?' Amber scowled, sticking out her chin and storming off after her mum.

Chapter 5

On the way home, Millie asked Mum if she could play in the park. It was still light out and Mum wanted to catch up with her friends too. They sprinted all the way to the swings, pretending to be super-speedy race cars.

Mum spotted Mrs Singh and they
started chatting, so Millie headed over
to the willow tree, where she knew the
Ballet Bunnies would be rehearsing for

their big show.

Millie's brush with Amber disappeared from her thoughts as soon as she saw Dolly *pirouetting* across the grass. The little bunny danced to the melody Fifi played on a tiny flute she had crafted out of a matchstick.

'Millie!' Pod called out, as she approached. 'Watch my magic trick.'

Pod swung his little magician's cape around his body. He held it out in front of him so just his ears could be seen over the top.

'Three, two, one . . .' he counted.

The cape dropped.

And Pod had completely disappeared! Millie gasped. *Where was Pod?*

He reappeared and laughed when he noticed Millie's mouth hung open in wonder.

'How did you do that, Pod?' Millie asked.

'It's supposed to be a secret,' Pod said. His nose twitched as he beckoned Millie closer. 'Don't tell anyone,' he whispered. 'But I run as quickly as I can before the cape drops so it looks like I vanish into thin air!'

'That's so clever,' Millie said, applauding Pod.

Trixie, who had been dozing in a shady spot, hopped over to join Millie and Pod.

Millie stroked Trixie's velvety fur. 'What will you be doing for the talent

show?' she asked the tiniest of
the four bunnies.

The sleepy bunny yawned. 'My special
skill is napping.'

Millie chuckled as Trixie squeezed herself into a teacup, and then into a large fern frond, and then into a pencil case, showing she, *in fact*, could absolutely sleep anywhere.

All four bunnies gathered together as
Millie cuddled them in a big snuggly hug.
She nuzzled into their soft fur and gave
their long silky ears a stroke each.

'How was class today?' Dolly asked.
'We were so busy rehearsing for the
talent show that we didn't make it to the
school.'

Millie told them all about the new
routine and how exciting it was to try
something more challenging. As she
spoke, Millie's smile turned into a frown.
She remembered Amber's mean words
and she told the bunnies what had
happened with Amber and her mum.

'It sounds like she has a lot to prove
to her Mum,' Fifi said.

'It's no excuse for being mean
though,' Dolly said.

41

The bunnies agreed. Before anyone could say anything more, Mum called for Millie. Hearing her mum's voice and seeing the bunnies around her, Millie felt very lucky to have the support she had.

◦ ✳ ◦

'I have something for you,' Mum said, plonking down on the grass next to Millie. The bunnies had darted behind the willow tree before Mum could spot them.

Mum handed Millie a shoebox-shaped parcel wrapped in a green ribbon.

Millie tore off the ribbon. She pulled off the top of the box and peered in.

It was a new pair of
tights and ballet shoes.
'Mum! They are
just like the ones
Precious has,' Millie
said, thinking of her
favourite ballerina of
all time.

'I want you to know, no matter what happens in the audition you have already made me so proud,' Mum said as Millie hugged her.

Millie couldn't wait. She slipped on the tights and shoes right there and stretched out her legs. At that moment, she felt like a professional ballet dancer.

She cuddled Mum tight again, and as she kissed her thank you, she saw her four Ballet Bunny friends grinning up at her from behind the tree. Millie felt her chest fill with warmth. She couldn't wait to work hard on her audition and show off her dancing in her beautiful new shoes.

Chapter 6

Millie tapped her feet on the wooden floor. It was audition day. She had on her new tights and shoes and she couldn't stop gazing down at them. She'd spent the last few days working really hard on her audition. She danced for Mum. She danced for the Ballet Bunnies.

She danced for her neighbour, Mrs Singh.

She even danced on the way to the shops.

Millie danced any chance she could get.

Mum had dropped her off at the town hall where the auditions were taking place. Dolly had snuck into Millie's ballet bag to come along too. Millie and Dolly watched the hall fill with young dancers. They stretched and warmed up and the low din of chatter started to get louder in the hall. Millie felt a flurry of nerves grow and swirl in her tummy.

'You'll be fine,' Dolly said, spotting Millie wringing her hands.

Millie managed a small smile but she didn't feel fine.

Millie and Dolly watched as Will was called to the dancefloor. He soared through the air and *pirouetted* with perfection. Will was good. He was really, really good. Millie desperately wanted to watch her classmate finish his routine, but the more she watched, the more her tummy hurt.

Could she ever dance
as well as Will?

53

Dolly tapped Millie with her paw. Her nose twitched towards an empty corridor that opened off the main hall. Millie scooped up the little bunny and they left Will's audition to head out to the quiet hallway.

'Is everything OK?' Dolly asked once they were alone.

Millie started to nod her head but it quickly turned to a shake of a no.

'It's so big,' Millie said. 'It's not like Miss Luisa's studio at all.'

The high ceilings and huge open space of the town hall made for an excellent audition space but it's cold intimidating size was nothing like Miss Luisa's cosy studio.

'It's just another place to dance,' Dolly reassured Millie. 'It's just another place to fill with your love for ballet.'

Dolly jumped out of Millie's hands and dove into Millie's ballet bag. She rummaged around inside before hopping back out to join Millie.

'Remember when you first joined Miss Luisa's school,' Dolly said. 'It was difficult, and you weren't sure you wanted to carry on dancing,' she continued. 'And remember how we spoke about how ballet made us feel like we were flying across clouds of candyfloss?'

Millie smiled. She remembered. She remembered struggling to keep up with the class at first. She remembered when she was just about to give up though, the ballet steps made sense and she felt like she was flying when she danced. She remembered finally making friends and

how much she loved ballet.

'I got you this,' Dolly said.

She handed Millie a small hairclip, decorated with a small tuft of pink tulle.

'It's the candyfloss hairclip you made me!' Millie exclaimed.

She slipped the clip into her hair and touched the fabric gently.

'Don't worry about what happens today,' Dolly said. 'Just go out there and dance like you are flying over candyfloss!'

ITIONS

Chapter 7

It was time for Millie's audition.

She took a deep breath and stepped out into the centre of the hall. She reached up to squeeze her hairclip and felt a burst of warmth in her chest. She knew, tucked away in a corner of the hall,

Dolly would be watching and cheering her on.

One of the judges counted Millie in and the audition music sounded. Millie took another deep breath and placed her feet into first position.

The rhythm flowed through Millie like paint on an easel. As the music built Millie's nerves melted away to nothing. She spun and jumped and *pirouetted* and *plied*, just like Miss Luisa had taught her.

Her ballerina dress floated around her like a silk ribbon in the wind. Millie soon forgot anyone was watching as she twirled faster and faster to the music. She couldn't help but smile the whole way through as she felt each note from the bottom of her toes all the way up to the tips of her fingers. And as she took her final jump, she soared through the air like she was flying over candyfloss.

Millie took a bow as the music died down. She saw the judges beaming at her and in that moment, she felt so proud of herself. She had remembered her steps and she had done her very best.

Millie stepped to the side as the judges made their notes and she saw that Amber was on next.

Amber had her arms wrapped tight around herself. Her skin was pale and she was trembling. Millie had never seen Amber like this. Amber was nervous.

'Good luck,' Millie said, smiling at her. She reached out to offer her a comforting hand but Amber pushed past her without even so much as a thank you.

Chapter 8

Millie watched as Amber
finished her routine, took a curtesy,
and then dashed off towards an empty
hallway. Millie followed after her.

'Amber?' Millie called out.

Muffled sobs were returned in reply.

Millie followed the sound to behind

a stack of chairs. She found Amber
huddled in a corner, crying into
her knees.

'Are you OK?' Millie asked,
crouching down to sit close to Amber.

Amber shook her head, so Millie searched her own bag for a spare tissue and offered it to her.

Amber looked up. 'Why are you being nice to me? I'm not very nice to you.'

Millie shrugged. 'You look really upset.'

Amber brushed away the tears from her wet cheeks. 'I wish I'd done better in my audition.'

Millie looked confused. 'But you were really good.'

'I don't think I was good enough,' Amber said, her voice small. 'And if I don't get the part, my mum will be really disappointed in me.'

'I don't think she will,' Millie said gently. 'I saw your audition. It was really, *really* good. I could tell you were trying your hardest.'

Amber curled up tighter into a ball but kept her eyes on Millie.

Millie remembered what *her* mum had said to her, 'All anyone can ask of you is to do your very best,' Millie said to Amber. 'You showed everyone out there how much you love ballet and that's all that matters.'

'I did,' Amber said, her
voice still tiny.

'You should tell your mum how you feel,' Millie continued.

'I don't think she'll understand,' Amber wept.

'You won't know unless you try,' Millie said. She put her arm around Amber's shoulder and gave her a squeeze.

Amber took a deep breath. She swallowed hard and nodded.

She sat up straight, pushed back her shoulders and wiped her tears away.

She put her arm around Millie and gave her a squeeze back.

'Thank you, Millie,' she said, sounding a little more like the

confident Amber Millie knew. She took
Millie's hands. 'I'm really sorry for being

mean to you.'

◦ ✳ ◦

Millie sat with Mum, holding her hand tight, as the audition results were announced. She felt in her pocket for Dolly who nuzzled back reassuringly.

Neither Millie nor Amber got the part. It went to Will.

Amber gave Millie a small smile and shrugged when the *Ballet Beat* judge announced Will's name. Millie watched from across the hall as Amber spoke to her mum. She felt a warmth in her chest again, like summer sunshine, when she saw Amber and her mum hug each other.

'Are you OK?' Mum asked Millie.

Millie nodded, though she couldn't help but feel a twinge of disappointment in the pit of her tummy.

'I'm so proud of you,' Mum said, hugging Millie tight. 'I think we deserve a trip to the park.'

Chapter 9

'Oh, bunny fluff,' Fifi said as Millie and Dolly joined them in the park. '*You* deserved that part, Millie,' she said.

'It's true,' Dolly said. 'You danced just as wonderfully as Will, so they could have easily picked you, Millie.'

Millie smiled. She *had* danced her

best and, as she thought back to her
audition, she realized just how proud she
was of herself.

'There will be lots of other parts to audition for,' Pod reassured her.

'You are the best bunny friends anyone could ask for,' Millie said.

She scooped them up in a huge hug and placed them down by a small stage set up beneath the willow tree.

Red, cloth napkins had been tied up to make curtains and smooth, flat stones had been set out in front of the stage as seats for the audience.

Fifi and Pod couldn't wait to introduce Millie round to all the Ballet Bunnies and Mambo Mice and Hip Hop Hedgehogs and Bhangra Blue Jays. Millie had to repeat everyone's name twice to try and remember all the wonderful new dancers she'd just met.

'I better get my seat,' Millie said to everyone. 'Your talent show is about to start!'

She wished each of them good luck and sat under the willow tree ready to watch the show.

Pod started the show with his vanishing trick and even though Millie

knew exactly what was going to happen,
she couldn't help but gasp with the
others when his cape dropped, and he
reappeared in the audience by the Hip
Hop Hedgehogs.

The Mambo Mice stunned everyone with their complicated dance routines and their glittery outfits. The Bhangra Blue Jays had everyone up on their feet, paws, and claws with a bhangra class to start off their routine.

But it was Dolly
who stole the show. Her
ballet routine was utterly magical.

She danced like she was painting a picture with her movements, sweeping the entire audience under her spell. And when Dolly was announced as the winner, Millie leapt to her feet with the other animals and cheered louder than anyone.

Dolly hopped straight over to Millie after she collected her trophy—a treble clef carved from a fallen branch.

'I'm so proud of how hard we have both worked this week,' she said to Millie.

'Me too,' Millie said, her chest swelling with pride.

Glossary of ballet terms

Barre – A horizontal bar at waist level on which ballet dancers rest a hand for support during certain exercises.

Demi – A small bend of the knees, with heels kept on the floor.

En pointe – Dancing on the very tips of your toes.

Jeté – A jump in which a dancer springs from one foot to land on the other with one leg extended outwards from the body while in the air.

Pas de deux – A dance for two people.

Pirouette – A spin made on one foot, turning all the way round.

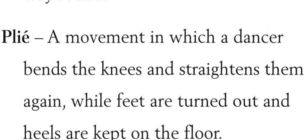

Plié – A movement in which a dancer bends the knees and straightens them again, while feet are turned out and heels are kept on the floor.

Relevé – A movement in which the dancer rises on the tips of the toes.

Sauté – A jump off both feet, landing in the same position.

About the author

Award-winning author Swapna Reddy, who also writes as Swapna Haddow, lives in New Zealand with her husband and son and their dog, Archie.

If she wasn't writing books, she would love to run a detective agency or wash windows because she's very nosy.

About the illustrator

Binny Talib is a Sydney based illustrator who loves to create wallpaper, branding, children's books, editorial, packaging and anything else she can draw all over.

Binny recently returned from living in awesome Hong Kong and now works happily on beautiful Sydney harbour with other lovely creative folks, drinking copious amounts of dandelion tea, and is inspired by Jasper her rescue cat.

If you enjoyed this adventure, you might also like . . .